너를 향해 사랑의 연鳶을 띄운다

Flying A Love Kite For You

그대는 누구이길래

고요히 앉아 있어도

속마음에 가득 차오르고

문을 닫아걸어도

가슴을 두드리는가

Who are you that fills up my heart,

even though I am sitting silently,

even though I lock the door of my heart?

Collected Poems on Love by Yong Chin Chong
(In Korean and English)

너를 향해 사랑의 연鳶을 띄운다
Flying A Love Kite For You

시
Poem

•

정용진
by Yong Chin Chong

•

그림
Picture

•

김난옥
by Nan Ok Kim

미래문화사

- 1939 - Born in Yeo - ju, Gyeong Gi - Do, Korea.
  Pen name "Soo Bong"
- president and Chairman of the Korean Literary Society of America
- Member of : the Association of Korean Writers for National Literature
- Member of : Pen U.S.A
- Advisor of the Orange Writers Group in the U.S.
- Winner of the Mijumunhak Award, the Korean Literary Society of America
- Winner of the Korea Christian Literary Award - Grand Prize
- Winner of the Editor's Choice Award, the International Library of Poetry
- Selected By The Best Poems & Poets Of 2005 From The International Library Of Poetry
- Poetry Books : "River Village" / "At the Rose Garden" / Filling the Empty Heart with Peace" / "Kum - Kang Mountain"
- Essay Books : "Planting the Meaning of Life" / "A Poet and a Farmer"

Email : yongc.chong@worldnet.att.net

Home Page : http : //myhome.mijumunhak.com/chongyongchin

Home Page : http : //myhome.naver.com/subong39

Translator Histories (영시로 번역한 사람들)

James Chong (정지선. 필자의 장남)

- Business Wire, Newsroom Supervisor
- University of California, Irvine - B.A. English, Phi Beta Kappa

Joseph Chong (정지민. 필자의 차남)

- eBay Inc., Product Manager
- University of Pennsylvania, The Wharton School of Business - M.B.A
- University of Pennsylvania, School of Engineering and Applied Science, M.C.I.T
- Harvard University - A.B. English and American Literature, Magna Cum Laude

Linda Kang Chong (정태경. 필자의 둘째 자부)

- Dodge & Cox, Analyst
- Goldman Sachs, Vice President
- Harvard Law School - J.D.
- Harvard University - A.B. Chemistry, Summa Cum Laude

John Roh (노정호. 필자의 조카)

- Columbia University, D.D.S
- University of California, Irvine - B.S. Biology

사랑은 아름답고
사랑은 따뜻하고
사랑은 행복하다
그러나 사랑은 때로는
외롭고 슬프고 아프다.

그대는 누구이길래
고요히 앉아 있어도
속마음에 가득 차오르고
문을 닫아걸어도
가슴을 두드리는가.

바람 부는 날
나는 너를 향해
사랑의 연鳶을 떠운다.

6

너는 문을 열고 나와
창공에 휘날리는 깃발을 보아라.

이 시집을 위하여 영역을 맡아준 아들 지신, 지민, 자부 태
령, 조카 정호에게 고마움을 표하고 정희성 시인과 김난옥
화백, 그리고 출판을 맡아주신 임종대 사장께 감사를 드린
다. 아내의 회갑을 기념하여 사랑의 시 71편을 추려 기쁜
마음으로 엮었다. 읽는 분마다 가슴속에 사랑이 넘쳐나기
를 진심으로 기원한다.

2006. 10월
San Diego 북부 Fallbrook, 에덴농장에서 저자.

Love is beautiful
Love is warm
Love is happy
But love is sometimes
lonely, sad and aching.

"Who are you that fills up my heart,
even though I am sitting silently,
even though I lock the door of my heart?"

On a windy day,
I am flying a love kite for you.

Open the door, dear,
and come out
and look up at the flag
dancing in the clear sky.

I give thanks to James, Joseph, Linda and John for
translating this book. I also give thanks to Lim Jong -
Dah for publishing it. To celebrate my wife's 60th
birthday, I organized this collection of love poems
with pleasure.

Yong Chin Chong

Fallbrook, North County San Diego, Eden Rose Farms

October 2006

7

8

2. 사랑의 기쁨 JOY OF LOVE

9

3. 사랑의 아픔 PAIN OF LOVE

10

4. 사랑의 추억 MEMORY OF LOVE

오늘도 나는

연연(戀戀)한

사랑의 실타래를 풀어

절절한 사연을

하늘 높이 띄운다

Today, again, I let out

the extended string of love

and send my affection high up

into the heavens

1.

사랑의 초대

INVITATION OF LOVE

사랑

그대는 누구이길래
고요히 앉아 있어도
속마음에 가득 차오르고

문을 닫아걸어도
가슴을 두드리는가.

내가 찾지 못하여
서성이고 있을 때
그대 마음도 그러하려니

차가운 돌이 되어
억년 세월을 버티지 말고
차라리
투명한 시내가 되어
내 앞을
소리쳐 지나가게나

골목을 지나는 바람처럼
바람에 씻기는 별빛같이

그대는 누구이길래
이 밤도 텅 비인 나의 마음을
가득 채우는가.

LOVE

I wonder who you are,
you who fill up the depth of my mind
while I keep sitting alone in silence.

You knock on my heart
even when I lock it tight.

You might be doing the same
when I roam about
looking all around for you.

Instead of a cold rock
standing upright beyond time,
may you rather become
a clear river
passing in front of me
with a splashing sound.

Like the breeze moving along an alley
as the starlight shining in the wind,
you charge my
whole empty soul tonight.
Wondrous you are.

15

징검다리

동구 밖을 흐르는
실개천에
뒷산에서 굴러온
바위들을
듬성듬성 놓아 만든
징검다리.

내가 서서
기다리는 동안
네가 건너오고,
네가 서서 기다리면
내가 건너가던
징검다리.

어쩌다
중간에서
함께 만나면
너를 등에 업고
빙그르르 돌아
너는 이쪽
나는 저쪽

아직도
내 등에 따사로운
너의 체온.

STEPPING STONES

The stepping stones
of the stream
running through the orchard
come from the back hills
from which they rolled.

While I wait,
you cross the stream
over these stones,
and while you wait,
I do the same.

Sometimes,
we meet in the middle.
I carry you on my back,
and turn you around,
and you go one way,
I go the other.

I can still feel
the warmth of your body
on my back.

님

내 그대를
그리워 하는 마음은
장미꽃 향이로라.

간밤 마른 땅을 적시며
함초롬히 내린
이슬비

길녘에는
줄지어 서서
나팔을 불며
사랑을 노래하는
연분홍 산나리꽃

개울 건너 떡갈나무 숲
꾀꼬리를 벗하여
동산에 오르면
하늘엔 눈부신 황금 햇살

면화 구름이
송이 송이
화장한 신부처럼 눈부시다

내 그대를
사랑하는 마음은
라반다의 향이로라.

LOVER

My heart
that yearns for you
is like the scent of a rose.

The drizzling rain
soaks the dry ground overnight.

Light pink flowers
are lined up and singing
songs of love, and playing the flute.

Crossing the stream
through a forest of oak trees,
the oriole is my friend
as I climb the hill.

The golden sunshine
radiates from the sky,
and floating cotton clouds
are gleaming like a bride
all made up.

My loving heart is like the scent
of lavender.

가을 아침에

그리워하는 마음
한 그루의 파초가 되어
내 가슴에
자라게 하옵소서

조그마한 생명의 빈 잔에
영원히 지워지지 않는
형상을 담아주시고
번뇌 없는 마음에
평정을 주옵소서

외로운 영혼
청자빛 하늘에
인생을 노 젓게 하옵소서

그날이 오면
희열에 넘치는
행복의 술잔을
당신 앞에 바치오리다.

찬란한 가을아침에
사랑의 노래를
들려주옵소서.

ONE AUTUMN MORNING

Let the yearning heart become
a lonely plant that grows
inside my heart.

Let the glass of life contain
an unforgettable figure,
and give peace to the
sufferless heart.

Let the lonely spirit
in the emerald-colored sky
row life.

When that day comes,
I will surrender the glass of
pleasure to you.

Let me hear the song of love
on this magnificent Autumn
morning.

연서戀書

간밤
문틈으로 스며드는
한기寒氣에
잠을 설치고

이른 아침
창을 여니
뜰 앞 감나무가
손을 내민다.

청명한 공간에서
첫서리를 맞으며
별들의 눈빛으로
밤새워
가슴속 깊이
아로새긴 연서戀書

진홍眞紅 글씨로
사랑이라 써 있다.
가슴이 뜨거웠다.

LOVE LETTER

Last night,
I could not sleep due to
the draft seeping through
the door gap.

In the early morning,
I open up the window.
The persimmon tree in the yard
reaches its hand to me.

I meet the first frost
in the clear air.
All night,
I carve my love letter
deep in my heart
with the light of the stars.

It says "love" in scarlet.
My heart is hot.

연鳶

바람 부는 날
나는
너를 향해
연鳶을 띄운다.

내 연연戀戀한
마음을 띄운다.

티 없이 연연涓涓한
그리움이
창을 두드리면

너는
문을 열고 나와
창공에
휘날리는 깃발을 보아라.

오늘도 나는
연연連延한
사랑의 실타래를 풀어
절절한 사연을
하늘 높이 띄운다.

* 연연戀戀 : 잊혀지지 않는 안타까운 그리움.
* 연연涓涓 : 시냇물이 졸졸 흐르는 모양
* 연연連延 : 죽 이어져 길게 벋음..

KITE

On a windy day,
I'm flying a love kite
for you.

My heart,
full of regrets,
I send up to you.

When the trickle of longing
knocks
at your heart's window,

open the door, dear,
and come out
and look up at the flag
dancing in the clear sky.

25

Today, again, I let out
the extended string of love
and send my affection high up
into the heavens.

아침기도

산은
얼마나 인仁 하기에
영원의 세월을 곤추서서
하늘을 우러르며

물은
얼머나 성품이 정淨하기에
돌 틈을 흐르며
저리 맑고 푸른가.

우주는
천, 지, 인, 의
아름다운 조화調和
산가에서
오늘의 일과를 열며

이 아침에도 향기
향기로운 차 한 잔을
앞에 놓고
감사하는 마음으로
주님을 향하여 부르는

나의
가난한 노래
절절한 기도여.

MORNING PRAYER

How patiently the mountain is facing the sky,
holding itself erect while
resisting the eternity of life.

How purely the water is murmuring
along the crevice in the rocks,
still and clear and blue as can be.

The universe,
the beautiful harmony of heaven, earth and man,
starts its daily routine at a cottage in the mountain.

Enjoying a cup of fragrant tea on the table
with a heart full of thanks,

I sing an ardent prayer,
my poor song.

외등

고독을 안으로 키우며
그 오랜 침묵

군중의 행렬이
멀어져간
뒤안길에서
허공을 향한
영원의 갈구

수녀의 기원을
닮는가

낙타의 갈증보다
더한 욕망으로

사랑의 철학을
역설하는
거리의 십자가.

LONELY STREET LAMP

Nurturing the loneliness,
that long silence

The marching crowd has long gone
from the alley where the street lamp stands.
It yearns towards the empty sky
and eternity

like a nun' s prayer,
desiring more than a camel' s thirst.

The cross of the street
emphasizes the philosophy of love.

봄달

날이 저물기를 기다려
달이
꽃에게 다가가서
너는
나의 입술이다 속삭이니

꽃이
달에게
너는 나의 눈썹이다
고백한다.

둘이
서로 마주보고
마음을 여니
향이 흐르고
미소가 넘쳐
봄밤이 짧더라.

SPRING MOON

Waiting for the day to end,
the moon goes to the flower and whispers,
"You are my lips."

The flower confesses to the moon,
"You are my eyelashes."

As they both look at each other
and open their hearts,
the scent is flowing and the smiles
are overflowing.
The spring night is brief.

석류꽃

내 짝꿍이
난蘭같이 귀엽던
소꿉친구
내 짝꿍이

대학 입학하던 첫날

석류꽃 같은
연지를 입술에 바르고
교문을 들어서다
들키자
화들짝 놀라!

그는 마침내
한 송이 붉은
석류꽃으로 피었다.

POMEGRANATE FLOWER

My childhood playmate,
as pretty as an orchid as we played house together,
my childhood playmate.

On the day I entered college,

she had on lipstick the color of a pomegranate
flower
and walked into school.
Upon spotting us,
her face filled with color and she feigned surprise.

She had finally blossomed,
like a cluster of deep red pomegranate flowers.

파피꽃

간 밤 새워 내린
봄비로
흙 가슴을 열고
솟아올라
노란 저고리
초록 치마를 걸치고
웃고 서 있는
애잔한 Poppy꽃.

나는
너에게로 다가가서
연인이 되어
사랑을 입 맞추고 싶다
이 푸른 아침에.

POPPY FLOWER

The spring rain that came during the night
opened up the earth,
from which blossomed the delicate poppy flower
wearing a yellow top and green skirt.
It stood sorrowfully,
and smiled.

I want to get close to you
and give you the kiss of love,
hoping that you will be my lover
this bright blue morning.

꽃노을

연지 찍고
곤지 찍고

간 밤
꿈길을 밟고
님 만나러 가는
구름 한 점.

서산마루를 오르다
발이 부르터
옷깃에 배인
붉은 꽃노을.

연지 찍고
곤지 찍고

그리움 품고 자란
내 아씨는
애련의 설움
옷고름에 썼고

저녁마다
수줍어
가슴 달아 오르는
붉은 꽃노을.

FLORAL SUNSET

Painting the cheeks red,
painting the forehead red,

a spot of clouds stepped
onto the road of dreams last night,
and is on its way to its lover.

It climbs the western mountain,
feet blistered,
and the red floral sunset
drenches its cloak.

Painting the cheeks red,
painting the forehead red,

my lady grew up with
a yearning heart, and washes
her tears of compassion on her
coat strings.

Every night,
shyness heats up the heart,
like a red floral sunset.

가을사랑

앞뜰에는
붉은
석류 두 알
뒤뜰에는
노을빛으로 타는
홍시.

이 모두
사랑스러운
너의 젖가슴이런만
터질까봐, 차마
만질 수가 없구나.

아!
이는 내가
이 가을에
너에게 보내는
순수
나의 첫사랑.

AUTUMN LOVE

In the front yard
are two red
pomegranates,
And in the back yard
burning in the color
of the sunset,
are persimmons.

These are all
your lovely breasts,
but as they may burst
I don' t dare to touch them.

O!
This is my
innocent first love
that I' m sending you
this Autumn.

나무 · 3

나는 너를 향해
너는 나를 향해

우리는
이렇게 서서
숲을 이루고
마주보며
팔을 벌려 껴안고
사랑에 빠진다.

너와 나의
깊은 가슴속에는
연륜마다 아롱져
출렁이는
사랑의
그윽한 물결.

TREE · 3

Me towards you,
You towards me

We are standing
like this,
forming a forest,
looking at each other,
arms outstretched,
embracing,
and fall in love.

In your and my
deep hearts,
mottled in every
annual ring,
are the lapping, quiet
waves of love.

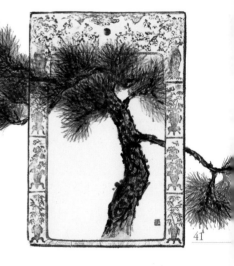

41

설야雪夜

사르륵
사르륵
잠든 대지 위에
눈발이 날린다.

햇이엉을 얹은
초가지붕 위에
포근히 쌓이는 눈송이들
솜이불처럼 따스하다.

내 가난한 심령은
토담집 화롯가에서
호젓이 잠들고
꿈결에
그리운 소녀가
사랑의 노래를 불러준다.

창밖에서는 아직도
소담스러운 함박눈이

사르륵
사르륵
내 영혼의 빈 잔을
가득히 채워준다.

NIGHT SNOW

Rustle
Rustle
Snowflakes are flying
over the sleeping ground.

On the new straw roof,
snowflakes are piling softly,
and they are as warm as
a cotton blanket.

My poor heart
is falling asleep gently
at the fireplace of a
mud-walled hut.
A girl yearning for
a dream is singing a
love song.

Outside of a window
large flakes of snow full-petaled,
juicy, ripe

Rustle
Rustle
are filling the empty cup
of my soul.

산울림

산에 올라
너를 부르니
산에서 살자 한다.

계곡을 내려와
너를 찾으니

초생달로
못 속에 잠겨 있는
앳된 얼굴.

다시 그리워
너를 부르니
산에서 살자 한다.

산에 올라
너를 부르니
산에서 살자 한다.

계곡을 흐르는
산들바람에

피어나는
꽃송이 송이들의
짙은 향기

다시 그리워
너를 부르니
산에서 살자 한다.

ECHO

When I climb up the mountain
and call out to you,
you say, "Let' s live here."

When I come down to the valley
and look for you,

I see your childlike face
in the pond
like the crescent moon.

When I miss you
and call out to you again,
you say, "Let' s live here."

When the gentle breeze
passes through the valley,

the strong scent of the flower buds
blossoms like the petals.

When I miss you
and call out to you again,
you say, "Let' s live here."

영월루迎月樓 · 2

오대산
굽이굽이 감돌아
흘러온 물줄기
여강驪江에 이르러
거울을 이루었구나

애타는 마음 한밤중
중천 명월로 떠서
내 가슴과
강심江心에
티 없이 푸르른데
연연戀戀한 그리움이
신륵사神勒寺 종소리로
물결져 흐르네.

밤마다
눈부시게
돌아오는 앳된 얼굴
그리운 임을

오늘도
가슴 가득 안으려
마암馬巖 영월루迎月樓
돌계단을 오르는
발자국 소리.

YOUNG WOL RU · 2

Oh Dae Mountain
A winding river at every turn
reaches the Yeo river
and forms a mirror.

In the middle of the night
my anxious mind rises
as a bright moon.
Affectionate yearning
flows as a stream
with the bell's ring of Sil Ruk temple
toward my heart and the heart of the river.

Every night
the baby-face rises brightly
My yearning lover

Today,
there is the sound of footsteps climbing
the stone steps of Ma Am Young Wol Ru,
trying to embrace its heart.

해금강

누구를 기다리다
선돌이 되었는가
타는 한恨
눈물로 고여
발 아래 출렁이는
애절한 물결소리.

아픔의 세월
임을 기다리다
망부석이 되었구나

오늘도
뜨거운 눈물을 식혀주는
실안개비

끼룩 끼룩
짝을 부르는
갈매기 떼들의
눈물겨운 갈구에

해금강은 오늘도
선돌로 서서
그리운 님을
저리 애절하게
기다리는구나.

HAE—GEUM RIVER

Who were you waiting for
that you turned into a standing stone?
The mournful river sound that
waves under my feet is
full of burning grief and tears.

In times of suffering,
as you wait for him,
you become Man-Boo Suk.

Today,
the threadlike rain
cools her burning tears.

With sad longing,
the flocks of seagulls
call for their mates.

The Heh-Geum River
once again stands as a stone
and waits for its lover,
full of longing.

사랑의 심장을 겨누는

화살촉

팽팽이 당겨져

활시위로 떠 있는 무지개

The arrow that is aimed at the heart of love

is tautly pulled against the rainbow

floating above it

2.

사랑의 기쁨
JOY OF LOVE

아내

아내는
꿈으로 깊어 가는
호수湖水

고요한 바람에도
가슴 설레이고
임을 기다리는
그리움으로
출렁이는 물결.

서러웠던
삶의 언덕에서
애처롭게 맺힌
눈물방울도

사랑한다는
한 마디 말에
소리 없이 녹아내리는
봄눈.

오늘도
인생의 기인 강가에 서서
그대를 부르면
노을빛으로 타오르는
사랑의 불빛

그대 가슴은.

WIFE

You, my wife, are like a lake
that deepens with a dream.

My heart trembles
even with the silent wind,
its yearning for you
disturbing the still waters.

On the hill of sorrows,
even the tears that swell
melt away like Spring snow
when you say "I love you."

Standing on the shore
of the river of life,
I call out to you
And the fire of my love
burns like the sunset

of your heart.

동백冬柏

1. 흰 동백

너의 순수는
순결의 상징.

푸른 물결이
몰려와 둘러섰다
버리고 떠나면
홀로 남는
섬의 외로움.

너는
태초 이브의 고독
숫처녀의 아픔이다.

2. 분홍 동백

너는
수줍은 영혼.

내 누님의
실눈 뜨는 첫사랑
동백기름의 윤기다.

가슴 뛰던
첫정이 부끄러워
서산 마루에 걸린
저녁노을

연지빛 사연
내 누님의
속가슴은.

3. 붉은 동백

타는 정열은
사랑의 혼불.

눈꽃이
하늘 가득 덮이는 날
비로서 신비의 문을 여는
황홀한
그 아픔.

이제 너는
여인으로
성숙하는구나

붉은
겨울 동백아!

CAMELIA

1. White Camelia

Your innocence is
a symbol of purity.

Blue water rushes in
and surrounds.
But when it is neglectful
and leaves, all that is left
is a lonely island.

You are the solitude
of Eve from the beginning,
the pain of a virgin maid.

2. Pink Camelia

You are a bashful spirit.

My older sister' s eye
opening up to first love
is the oil of the camellia
glistening.

Embarrassed by the first love
that used to make my heart race,
the sunset hangs from the floor
of the west mountain,
circumstances tinted rouge
from my older sister' s heart.

3. Red Camelia

Burning passion is
the soul fire of love.

Snowflakes cover the sky,
even though the rapture of pain
opens the door of mystery.

Now you have matured into a lady,
red winter camellia.

초승달

어제 밤
오랜만에
아내와 함께
산책을 나섰다.

서녘 하늘
고목에 걸린 달이
하도 애처로워
살짝 떠다가
창가에 걸어 두고
꿈결에 들었더니

이른 새벽
아내의 이마 위엔
아스라이
초승달이 걸려 있고

내 코밑엔
솔개 한 마리가
날고 있었다.

CRESCENT MOON

Last night I went walking with my wife
for the first time in a while.

A crescent moon that was hanging from
an old tree against the west sky
was so fragile that I scooped it up
and hung it on my window.
Then, I fell into my dream world.

In the early morning, the crescent moon
was hanging below my wife's forehead.
And beneath my nose, the same black eagle
was soaring.

61

달

흰구름 사이로
연인의 눈썹 같은
몸매를 들어내는
소녀여

모두가 잠든
대지 위에
너 홀로
잠 못이루는가

청산을 그리는 너는
외로운 시인의 고향이어라.

MOON

Between the white clouds,
shaped like a lover's eyebrow,
your figure is revealed,
Oh, my darling!

While all on earth sleep,
you are the only one sleepless.

You are painting the evergreen mountain.
You are a lonely poet's hometown.

달 · 2

텅 빈 하늘에
어두움이 덮여 오면
달이 달이
해맑고 푸른 달이
님의 창가를
찾아오네.

오다가 지치면
고목에 걸터앉아 쉬고
맑은 호수에서
둥근 얼굴을 씻네

구름은
시녀로 거느리고
님을 찾아오네

덩달아 따라나서는
은하수와
별들의 무리.

님 그리워서
낮에는 졸고
밤을
칠흑의 밤을 기다려
천지사방이 잠들 때
님의 창가를
찾아오네.

MOON · 2

When the darkness covers up the empty sky,
the moon, the moon,
the clear blue moon is
arriving at your window.

If the moon gets tired during its travels,
it sits on the old tree and rests.
It washes its round face in the clear lake.

The moon comes to you
with the clouds as her servants.

The Milky Way and
the halo of stars
also follow along.

During the day, the moon
naps and longs for you.

During the night, the black
dark night, when all is asleep,
the moon comes by your window.

무지개

봄을 여는
아침비로
혼을 씻은 하늘

겹겹이 쌓인 연서를 들고
머리를 곱게 빗은
색동 아씨가 웃고 있다.

사랑의 심장을 겨누는
화살촉
팽팽이 당겨져
활시위로 떠 있는 무지개

그것은 위협
그것은 과시
그것은 약속이었다.

맑게 씻긴
티 없는 가슴에 안겨
운우雲雨의 정을 나누는
사랑의 뜨거운 밀어

아!
그 석류 속 같이
붉게 타는 연정.

RAINBOW

The morning rain opens up the Spring,
and washes the soul of the sky.

Carrying piles of love letters
and combing her hair,
the young woman is smiling.

The arrow that is aimed at the heart of love
is tautly pulled against the rainbow
floating above it.

That was the threat
That was the display
That was the promise

The cleanly washed, unblemished heart
is embraced by the sweet whispers
of a lover sharing the emotions of cloud and rain.

O burning love
like the inside of a pomegranate!

고독

서산을 가리운
붉은 노을은
내 창가에
또하나의
고독을 달아주고

머언 강언덕엔
그리운 밀어들이
전설처럼 흐르는
이국의 여름밤

그대는
어떤 추억을
가슴 깊은 곳에
탑처럼 쌓는가.

멘델스존의
선율보다도
더 조용히 흐르는
세월…

창밖에서
서러운 얼굴을 들어내고

눈물을 참아가며
호올로 외로운
보름달

내 아내의
얼굴이여.

SOLITUDE

The red sunset
that covers the western mountain
hangs solitude once again
at my window.

At the far hill,
yearning lovers' whispers
flow like a myth in the summer night
of a foreign country.

What kind of memories
do you pile up like towels
in the depths of your heart?

Time
that flows
more quietly than
Mendelssohn's melodies

Outside the window,
the lonely, full moon
reveals its sorrowful face
and holds back its tears.

O my wife's
lovely face!

장미

새벽 안개
면사포로 드리우고
그리움 망울져
영롱한 이슬
방울 방울.

사랑이
가슴에 차오르면
비로서
아름 아름 입을 여는
장미꽃 송이 송이들.

사납게 찌르던
가시의 아픔도
추억의 향기로 번지는
꽃그늘 언덕에서
뜨거운 혼불로
타오르는 밀어여.

ROSE

The morning fog arrives like a veil.
The yearning heart buds into morning dew.
Drip, drop

When love fills up within the heart,
the buds open their mouths one by one.
Bloom, bloom

Even the pain from the piercing thorn
diffuses like the scent of remembrance,
and burns like a blazing fire at the
hill of the flowery shade.

사과꽃

나른한 윤사월
따가운 햇살 받아

진흙 딛고
도리桃李인 양
홀로 수줍은
사과꽃.

어려서는 푸른 볼이
과년하여
꿈빛으로 익어

서녘 하늘
황혼을
타는 저녁 노을
빠알간 가슴.

APPLE BLOSSOM

In the drowsy April,
you receive the warm sunshine.

A lonely apple blossom
is standing in the mud
like a peach and plum.

The green cheek that you had
when you were young, has passed
and ripened like a dream.

The sunset with a red,
scarlet heart burns the dusk
in the west sky.

73

자카렌다

자카렌다
신비의 여신이
오월의 문을 연다.

누님의
소맷자락같이
치렁 치렁 늘어진
보랏빛 옷자락

가슴속엔
청자 항아리의
천 년 얼이
출렁이고

사랑을 갈구하던
연인들이
자카렌다 그늘
그윽한
호심에 안겨
석류꽃 같은
입을 맞춘다.

JACARANDA

Jacaranda.
The goddess of mystery
opens the door of May.

Like my older sister's dress sleeve,
the stretched out purple hem
hangs loosely.

Within the heart,
a thousand year-old spirit
is wading in a green vase.

Lovers who are craving love
are embraced in the shade of the Jacaranda
like the center of a lake,
and touch lips that are like a
pomegranate flower.

산정호수山井湖水

흐르는 세월 머물러
천 년 햇살 빛나고

갈바람 멎어
산 그림자를 담는
너는
하나의 거울

하늘 기려
솔개보다
깊푸른 눈매로
가냘픈 멧새의
숨결에도
가슴 떨어
붉게 물드는 마음이여.

내 뜻 청산되어
너를 품어
태고의 신비를 묻는
가을 한낮

초연한 걸음으로
산을 넘는
한 줄기 푸른 구름.

A LAKE ON TOP OF THE MOUNTAIN

Flowing time stops;
The 1,000 year sun shines.

A wind that is about to pass
contains the shadow of a mountain.
You are a mirror.

You are deeper than an eagle' s eyes.
My heart is shaken even by
the weak tomb bird' s breath.
O my heart, dyed in red!

My will becomes a
green mountain that embraces
the mystery of beginning,
which is buried on this
warm Autumn afternoon.

A blue cloud is strolling
alone, climbing the mountain.

여강驪江

님은
명주 비단자락.

내 마을 인정을
살포시 두르고
굽어 도는
청실 강줄기
그리운 물결소리

밤마다
애틋한 꿈을 싣고 와
은모랫벌
조포潮浦 나루를 건너는

님은
아련한 달빛.

내 누님의
속마음 같은
명주 비단자락.

* 여강은 여주 앞강 이름.
* 조포는 신륵사 앞 나루 이름.

YEO RIVER

Darling,
you are a river of silk.

Enveloped by the warm
heart of the town,
it curves like a blue thread.
I long for the running sound.

Every night, the river brings
yearning, affectionate dreams,
and ferries over the silver,
sandy field of Joh-Poh port.

Darling,
you are a distant beam
of moonlight.

The river is like my older sister's
heart-a gossamer
drape of silk.

강江나루

노을 붉어
하루가 저무는
강江나루.

계곡을 따라 흐르는 종소리
종소리를 따라 내리는 강물

천만 길 벼랑을
구르는 아픔보다
더한 진통의 밤은
침묵의 산을 낳고

청명한 공간에 삶을 부르면
티 없이 메아리져
되돌아 오는 언덕에서

온갖 번뇌로 젖어온
그 마음은

바람을 따라 흐르는 종소리
종소리를 따라 내리는 강물

가오는 세월도
맴돌아 씻기는 길녘에 서면
님의 노래는
애달픈 물결

오늘도
머언 꿈길을 밀어가는
강나루.

RIVER DOCK

The sunset reddens
and the day is ending
at the river dock.

The sound of the bell travels
down the deep valley
and the river travels alongside it.

The night of suffering is more painful
than rolling down the long road
and gives birth to a mountain of silence.

If I call out to life into the clear sky,
it echoes back perfectly to the hill
upon which I am standing.

And my heart is drenched
with all suffering

81

The sound of the bell follows
the wind, and the river follows
alongside it.

Your singing is like the agonizing waves,
as time swirls and stops at the dock.
The river dock pulls forth the dream
once again, today.

나무 · 4

너와 나는
깎아지른 산비탈에 서서
네 뿌리로
내 발등을 덮고
내 팔로
너의 어깨를 감싸며
힘든 세상을 이겨나가자.

차가운 하늘
눈이 내리면
호호백발 노인으로 서 있다가
다시 햇살이 비치면
싱그러운
소년 소녀로 되돌아와
함께 사랑을 노래 부르자
낭떠러지 산비탈에
푸르게 서서.

TREE · 4

You and I
are standing on the steep
mountain slope.
Your roots cover the
top of my foot.
My arm is draped
over your shoulder.
Let's go forward and
beat this hard life.

When the cold sky
snows, you stand
as a white-haired old man.
If it rains again,
you come back as a fresh
boy and girl,
and let's sing a love song
together,
standing greenly
at the mountain slope.

산행山行

낙엽이 지는 소린가 싶어
계곡을 찾아드니
외진 숲속에서
꽃이 피고 있었다.

빈손으로
찾아간 나에게
그는
향기를 전해 주고
웃음은 덤으로 준다.

나도 그대에게
무엇인가 주고 싶어
찾았으나 빈손뿐

겸연쩍게 돌아서는데
지나던 바람이
향을 싣고 따라와
옷깃에 뿌려 준다.

그대가 오는 소리인가 싶어
귀를 기울이니
꽃이 지고 있었다.

MOUNTAIN TRIP

I went to the valley because I thought
I heard the sound of falling leaves,
but it was the blooming of flowers
deep in the forest.

I went searching
with empty hands,
and he gave me scents
and an abundance of smiles.

I went because I wanted to
give him something,
but I was empty-handed.

As I was returning, ashamed,
passing winds followed me
carrying scents, and soaked
my clothes.

I strained to listen
because I thought you were coming,
but saw that the flowers were already wilting.

농부의 일기

나는
마음의 밭을 가는
가난한 농부.

이른봄
잠든 땅을
쟁기로 갈아

꿈의 씨앗을
흙가슴 깊숙이
묻어 두면

어느새
석양빛으로 영글어
들녘에 가득하다.

나는
인생의 밭을 가는
허름한 농부.

진종일
삶의 밭에서
불의를 가려내듯
잡초를 추리다가

땀 솟은
얼굴을 들어
저문 하늘을 바라보면
가슴 가득 차오르는
영원의 기쁨.

DIARY OF A FARMER

I am
a poor farmer
plowing the field of my heart.

Early in the Spring,
I plow
the sleeping land.

If I bury the seeds
of the dream
in the deep heart of the soil,

soon, in no time,
it ripens as the color
of the falling sunset,
and fills the field.

I am
a shabby farmer
plowing the field of life.

All day, in the field
of life, I sort out
the weeds, like I
sort out injustice.

I raise my sweaty face
and look at the evening sky,
and the happiness of eternity
fills my heart.

나의 시詩

나의 시는
한밤중
야래향夜來香이 번지는
뒤뜰을 거닐다가

문득 마주친
연인의 가슴속에서
건져낸 아픔이다.

빈 들에
눈발이 덮이듯
낙엽이 쌓이는
늦가을
돌계단을 오르는
발자국소리다.

나의 시는
한겨울
동면의 시간들을
인내로 살다가
언 땅을 가르고 솟는
생명의 열기.

이제
가난한 마음속에
영혼의 깃발로
나부끼는 감격이다.

푸른
심원深遠에서
끝없이 출렁이는
물결소리다.

MY POEM

My poem is like
strolling in
the backyard where the
night fragrance spreads,

and suddenly encountering
your lover and pulling
the pain from her heart;

like snowflakes spreading,
and fallen leaves piling up
in the empty field;
like the stepping sound
of footsteps going up the
stone stairs.

My poem is like
the heart of life that
comes from the frozen soil,
patiently, after the winter sleep.

But now,
it is like the waving inspiration
of the flag of the soul of a poor heart.

And it is like
the endlessly flowing sound of
blue water.

지금은 낙엽이 되어

망각의 뒤안길을 외롭게 딩구는

사랑의 언어들

It has become a fallen leaf,

and rolling on the street of forgetfulness

are lonely words of love

3.

사랑의 아픔

PAIN OF LOVE

춘설春雪

지난 가을
늦서리에 잎 떨구고
찬 하늘에 몸 얼어
봄꿈 그립던 나목裸木

간밤 춘설에
가지마다 꽃을 달고
웃는 얼굴

뜨락에는
내 누님의 동정 같은
달빛으로 피어나는
봄눈의 향기.

SPRING SNOW

Last Fall,
a bare tree that was yearning
for the Spring dream was
dropping leaves from
the late frost,
and the body was frozen
because of the cold sky.

Last night,
because of the Spring snow,
from each branch hung
a flower, and the bare tree
had a smiling face.

In the field,
the scent of the Spring snow
blossomed in the moonlight,
like my sister's compassion.

나무의 연가戀歌

나무는
산이 좋아
산에서 산다.

새들이
곁에 와서
노래를 불러주면
간간히 손을 흔들어줄 뿐

스스로 꽃을 피워
향을 발하고
시냇가에 발을 담근 채
밤마다
별들과 대화를 나누는
외로운 나무.

늦가을
산심山心이 그리워
찾아오실 임을 기다리다
길역에 서서

간밤
찬서리에
가슴이 붉어
홀로
수줍은 연인아.

A TREE'S LOVE SONG

A tree
lives in the mountain
because it likes it.

When the birds
come by and sing,
sometimes the tree waves.

The tree, by itself, lets the
flowers blossom and
release their fragrance.
As it dunks its feet
in the stream at night,
the lonely tree has a
conversation with the stars.

Late Autumn,
yearning for the soul
of the mountain,
the tree stands by the street
waiting for its lover to come

Last night's
cold frost
dyes its heart red.
O you lonely,
shy lover.

장미가시

장미농장을 경영하면서
제일 먼저 친해진 것은
사나운 가시다.

사랑을 받으려면 먼저
사랑을 보내야 하는 것처럼
껴안으면
가슴을 찌르고
어루만지면
손바닥에 박힌다.

그것은
미모와 향기의 이면에
깊숙이 숨겨둔 비수匕首

우리 내외는
밤마다 돋보기 안경을 끼고
뾰족한 바늘로
나는 아내의 손에
아내는 나의 손에 든
가시를 파낸다.

어떤 한의사는

가시에 찔리면
수지침手指針을 맞는 효험이 있어
장수할 거라고 위로하기에

우리 내외는 아픔을 꾹 참고
크게 웃었다.

오늘도
장미가시가
혼미한 세상 속에서
나를 파낸다.

ROSE THORNS

As I farm the roses,
the first thing that I encounter
are the aggressive thorns.

If one wants to be loved
one should first send love,
painful as it is;
just as when I embrace the roses
the thorns pierce my chest,
or when I caress them,
they pierce my palms.

That is the pain
hidden behind the beauty and
fragrance of roses.

Each night, my wife and I
put on our glasses and
dig the thorns out from each
other's hands with a sharp needle.

An acupuncturist comforted us
by saying that each time

we get poked by a thorn,
it has the effect of acupuncture
and will increase our lifespan.

And so we laugh loudly
and suppress our pain.

Today, the rose thorns
dig me out
from the uncertainty
of life.

산머루

꽃사슴도
입맞추는
숲길 사이로
조각 하늘이 열리면

그리움 못견뎌
고목 등걸을 휘감던
산머루가 익는다.

바람이
세월로 흐르고
세월이
바람으로 흐르는
외진 산록.

길 찾는
너의 옷빛도
주홍으로 물들고

머루향에 취한
이 저녁
산노을이 붉다.

WILD GRAPES

The sky opens upon
the meadow where
the deer couple meet.

The wild grapes cannot
resist the yearning,
and ripen as they curl up
from the back of the old tree.

The wind flows as time,
and time flows as the wind
on this lonely mountain.

As you look for the
mountain road,
your clothes are dyed
in scarlet.

Drunken by the scent
of wild grapes,
the sunset is so red
this evening.

산 노을

생명은
사랑의 마음이라
그리워함이 있어

고통하며
번뇌하며
찾아 방황하나니

어쩌면
젊은날의
맑고 푸른 그 눈길
아늑한 정情

속 가슴이
타오르고 타올라
싱그러운 육신은
그윽히 감추우고

임을 부르던
수줍은 입술만 남아
저녁마다 저리
붉은 열기로
번져 오르는가

기인
산 그늘에
들길이 안기우고

까마귀 떼들도
계곡을 맴돌아
찬 숲에 내리는
어스름.

비가 오려나
저녁 연기도
솔잎 내음으로
뽀오얗게
들길을 덮는
외진 산마을

그리움의 강심엔
사랑의 물결이 일고

외로운 가슴을
소리 없이 젖어드는
붉은 산노을.

MOUNTAIN SUNSET

Life
is the heart of love
because there is yearning.

In pain,
in agony,
searching, wandering.

Perhaps,
on a young day,
the clear blue line of sight
is a comfortable love.

The heart within
burns and burns.
The fresh body is hidden
quietly.

Only left with the shy
lips that call to the lover;
every evening it rises
with the red heat.

The long
mountain shadow
covers the field road
and a flock of crows.

Swirling around the valley,
the dusk lands
on the cold forest.

Perhaps it will rain.
The evening smoke
of the scent of the pine needles
from the lonely mountain village
covers the field road.

At the center of the
river of yearning,
the waves of love
begin.

The red mountain sunset
silently soaks in
the lonely heart.

무제無題

싱그러운 미래의 꿈을
남향한 언덕에 가꾸며
숱한 밀어를 익혀오던
동구밖 과원

한 알의 사과를 잉태하자던
아름다운 염원은
산산이 조각나고

지금은 낙엽이 되어
망각의 뒤안길을 외롭게 딩구는
사랑의 언어言語들

물빛보다 차가운 그대의
눈망울 눈망울

언 가슴을 따스히 녹여주던
부드러운 손길
이제는 돌아올 수 없는
애별리고愛別離苦의
운명과 손잡고

머얼리 멀리
떠나 가는가

눈물 없는 이별을
아름다운 슬픔을.

UNTITLED

Cultivating
the dream of a fresh future
on the south-headed hill,
the orchard
has hidden so many lovers' whispers

The desire to conceive an apple
has been completely demolished

It has become a fallen leaf,
and rolling on the street of forgetfulness
are lonely words of love

Your eye, your eye
is colder than the light of water

Your touch
that used to melt my frozen heart

Now
we are hand in hand with the
fate of suffering from separation
and leaving for faraway lands

For separation without tears
For beautiful sadness

이별離別

황혼이
달무리처럼 깔리는
골목길을
구르는 낙엽은
저문 길손.

그는
삶의 아픔들을
진홍으로 엮어놓고

외진
포구를 찾아가

낡은 목선에
몸을 싣는다.

차가운 강물에는
구름이 떠 있고
바람이 불고
세월이 흐른다.

떨어져 나가는
지체를 바라보며
구부정한 허리를
내어 보이는
고목 잔등에는

달빛이 흐르고
눈물이 있고
추억이 슬프다.

PARTING

Dusk carpets the street
like a halo.
Fallen rolling leaves
are a traveler who
has reached the end.

He embroiders
the pain of life
in scarlet.

He searches
the lonely port

and gets aboard
the old
wooden vessel.

Clouds float upon
the cold river;
the wind blows;
time passes.

Looking at the tree' s
limbs falling away,
he spies its slightly
curved back.

Moonlight flows,
tears fall,
memories ache.

낮달

간밤을 뒤척이다
뜬눈으로 지새우고
해가 중천임을
아득히 잊은 채
소리 없이 사위어가는
하아얀 낮달.

돌아서서 떠나가던
옛 님의
고운 뒷모습이
낮달로 떠오르면

가을 강처럼
깊게 깊게 고여 오는
마알간 하늘

회상의 물결이
굽이굽이 아롱지는
푸른 호반에는

박꽃 같은 몸매로
소리 없이 낡아가는
그대의 얼굴
하아얀 얼굴.

DAY MOON

I lay awake tossing and turning
all night long.
I am unaware that mid-day has passed
until I see the day moon silently fading.

When the elegant image of you as you leave
appears as the day moon,
the clear sky fills up like an autumn river
deeper and deeper.

Waves of recollection are coloring
every undulation
of the blue lakeshore.

Your face like a white day moon,
ages silently with the figure
of a gourd flower.

비오는 창가에서

비오는 창가에서
빗소리를 들으며
유리창이 씻기는 모습을 바라다보면

가냘픈 내 영혼도
수정처럼 맑게 씻기는
기쁨을 얻는다.

산길을 덮으며 눈이 오던 날
가슴 가득 차오르던 충만감

땅거미가 내리는 어스름
봉당을 올라서며 눈을 털던
발소리가 그립다.

비오는 날엔
온종일
잊혀진 사람의 소식이
기다려진다.

빗물이 흐르는 창밖에
유채화로 서 있는
너의 얼굴

아직도 창밖에는
귀에 익은 발소리처럼
저벅저벅
비가 나리고 있다.

BY THE WINDOW

As I stand by the window
and listen to the rain and look
at the glass being washed,

my delicate soul,
cleansed crystal clear,
is happy.

On the day the falling snow
covers the mountain road,
satisfaction fills my heart.

As I cross the dirt floor
during dusk, I reminisce
about the times when I used
to shake the snow from my feet.

On rainy days, I wonder about the people
I have forgotten.

Outside the window,
your face stands as an
oil painting.

Like familiar footsteps,
rain is still falling outside
the window.

119

도라지꽃

누님의 무덤같이
나직한 산기슭

이른 아침
눈물 같은
이슬을 달고
깨어나서

간밤
애태우던
꿈을 노래하는
백도라지꽃
떨리는 숨결.

노을이 붉게 번지는
머언 산마루엔
목이 타는
사슴의 무리들.

그대의 설움 배인 발소리가
옷깃을 스치며
가슴에 와닿아

애닯게 흘러간
인연의 시간들을
회상하는
자색 도라지꽃
슬픈 몸짓.

BELL FLOWER

The base of the mountain
is like my older sister's
tombstone.

It awakens with tear-like
dew drops in the early morning.

The trembling breath of the
white bell flower sings
the yearning dream last night.

Flocks of deer are thirsty
at the mountain top that
spreads out in redness.

Your footsteps soaked with sorrow
swiftly touch the tip of my cloak
and my heart.

The purple bell flower moves sadly,
remembering the lovers' happy times
that have passed anxiously by.

박꽃

솔 숲을 가르는
천 년의 바람 한 점
성하盛夏에도 설경雪景으로
가지마다
학鶴이 내려

선비의 지조로
그윽한
솔의 향기.

외진 산모롱이
돌담길을
살포시 돌아서면

초가지붕마다
누님의 동정같이
하아얀 달빛으로
피어나는 박꽃.

GOURD FLOWER

A whiff of wind,
which could have blown through the pine forest
for thousands of years
Cranes landing on branches
decorated with snow,
even in midsummer

Scent of pine,
full of fragrance,
representing the motto and
principle of a scholar

Turning along a lone lane,
paralleled by a stone wall and
leisurely curved

Fields of gourd flowers are seen
on every thatched roof of straw,
flowers moon-shone like the white collar
of my sister's traditional dress

패랭이꽃

외진 길녘에 밟히며 살아온
패랭이꽃.

기다리는 세월이 서러워
흐르는 한 순간이 마음 아파라

아침 노을에
두 뺨이 붉었구나

그대가 서럽게 울던 자리에
밤마다 별빛이 가득.

엉겅퀴 손톱에 할퀴운 두 볼을
흐르는 바람이 씻어준다.

외진 길녘엔
천민의 혼으로 서 있는
애닲은 너의 모습
패랭이꽃.

잘 자거라 이 밤을
기다리던 님이 네 품에 돌아와
고운 꿈길을 엮어주리라.

WILD PINK

Wild pink
you have lived a life of being stepped upon,
on the isolated road

Sorrowed by your painful wait,
a moment passing is heartache.

Your cheeks are reddened
by the morning sunset.

There are nights filled with stars
where you are mourning in grief.

The streaming wind cleanses and heals
the cheek scratched by wild thistles.

Your figure is sorrowful,
standing alone like the spirit of a slave
on the isolated road.

Goodnight.
The lover waiting for tonight
will come back to your embrace
and knit your beautiful dream road.

들꽃

천 년의 정적이
낡은 시간들처럼
소리 없이 쌓이는
후미진 산록에
홀로 서서
임을 기다리는
들꽃 한 송이.

지나는 바람결에
가슴 떨며 손을 흔들고
애타는 마음을
향으로 피워내는
외로운 들꽃.

아침 햇살에
노을빛 색동옷을
가려입고
볼 붉히는 너는
순결의 화신化身

애틋한 사연을
유채화로 담아
청산에 둘러두고

오늘도
그리운 임을 기다리는
슬픈 들꽃아.

WILD FLOWER

The silence of 1,000 years
is quietly piling, like old times
in the deep part of the mountain.
A wild flower is standing by itself,
lonely, waiting for a lover.

The passing wind trembles its heart
and shakes its hands.
A lonely wild flower
releases the scent of a yearning
heart.

With the morning sunshine,
you' re wearing clothes with
stripes of many colors,
and blushing like a goddess
of innocence.

You contain heartrending stories
in the oil painting of the
blue mountains near you.
O! you sad wild flower,
waiting for your lover again
today.

나목裸木

그리워 애탄가슴
님찾아 떠돌다가
길잃어 잎떨구고
너홀로 선자리에
차가운 서릿바람
돌아와 서성이네
구르는 낙엽소리
가을이 깊었는가.

낯익은 동산떠나
그대를 찾았노라
부르는 그음성이
티없이 메아리져
아련한 추억들이
들길에 번지는데
그대의 발자국에
가을이 쌓여있네.

BARE TREE

Yearning, sorrowful heart,
searching for my lover, wandering,
and I get lost, and leaves are lost.
Where you stand alone,
there is a frosty wind
that comes and paces restlessly.
The sound of fallen leaves rolling.
O the deepening Autumn!

I left the familiar hills
and searched for you.
The voice that calls for you
echoes cleanly.
Hazy memories spread out
over the field.
Autumn piles up
on your footprints.

석양

떠나는 마음
애닲어
하늘에는 꽃구름
장미빛 꽃구름.

가는 님 서러워
여인의
하아얀 머플러 위로
붉게 물드는
수줍은 속마음.

솔개는
텅 비인 산마루를
외로이 맴돌고
저문 하늘에는
장미빛 꽃구름.

EVENING SUNSET

The heart leaving,
aches.
A flower cloud in the sky,
rose-colored

The lover leaving is sorrowful;
the heart inside dyed in red
over the lover's white muffler

The black kite
flies in a lonely circle
around the empty mountain.

The evening sunset,
clad in red clothes,
moves in steps, aloof.

A rose-colored flower cloud
in the evening sky

단풍丹楓

지금
줄리안 계곡에는 고목 가지마다
옮겨 붙는
불빛이 한창이다.

잎들은
그 영혼이 얼마나 투명하기에

한밤중
별들이 쏟아 놓은 눈빛만으로도
연정의
타는 입술로 저리 붉었는가.

순간을 살아도 영원으로 물드는
나무들의 침묵의 언어들……

서릿발이 영그는 하늘
땅거미가 내리는 어스름

다리를 절고 가는 여인의
발자국 위로
추억이 소리 없이 쌓이고 있다.

* 줄리안은 샌디에고 팔로마 산자락의 단풍이 아름다운 사과동산.

BURNING LEAVES

Now,
in the Julian Valley,
beams of sunlight spread
on each branch of the old tree.

How deep and clear
is the soul of the leaves

that they become so reddened
by the burning lips of love,
lit by the beams of starlight.

The silent language of the trees
is dyed in red forever, though
the trees themselves last momentarily.

The skies are ripened with frost.
The dusk descends upon
the darkness.

Memories silently pile up
in the uneven footsteps of a
crippled woman's walk.

*Julian Valley is a beautiful apple hill in San Diego's Palomar
Mountain.

설한부雪寒賦

초겨울 눈송이들이
마른 가지 위로
고기비늘처럼
번쩍이며 나리는데

새끼들이 잠든 동굴
길을 잃은
늑대의 울음소리가
계곡을 가른다.

바람을 앞세우고
흰 도포자락을 휘날리며
산을 내려오는
차가운 달.

창 틈으로 스며드는
한기에 젖어
옛님의 숨결로 떨고 있는
촛불이 애처롭다.

한 세기를 잠재우고
새 시대를 일깨우는
여명黎明

지금쯤
어느 곳에서
태반의 아픔을 찢고
또 하나의 생명이
탄생하는가.

POEM FOR THE COLD SNOW

In the early winter,
snowflakes come down
like the shiny scales of a fish
onto the dry branches.

In the cave
where the young sleep,
the cries of lost wolves
pierce through the valley.

The cold moon
pushes the wind that
makes white clothes flutter,
and tumbles down the mountain.

The sad candlelight
is soaked by the winter air
and shaken by the breath of an old lover.

The dawn
wakes up a new Century,
wakes up a new era.

About now,
where is a new life born,
a painful breaking of the placenta?

* winner of the Korean Christian Literature Grand Award

135

이제

머언 길을 떠난

그대가

상념의 낙엽을 밟고

되돌아와

석류 같은

입술을 포개어

사랑을 입맞출 때

Now you are returning from the long trip,

stepping on leaves of ideals.

When I exchange a kiss of love

with your lips of pomegranate

4.
사랑의 추억
MEMORY OF LOVE

강마을

내 님이 사는 마을은
돛단배 밀려오고
따사로운 인정 머무는
버들숲 강마을.

동산에 돋는 해 머리에 이고
가녀린 손길을 모두어가며
한없이 한없야 기다리는 마음

애달픈 사연 토해놓고
기러기 떼 떠나가고
파아란 강심에 깃드는 강노을

하아얀 모래밭 푸른 갈숲을
끝없이 끝없이 가고픈 마음

외로운 초생달 창가에 들면
멧새도 울음 멈춰 숲으로 드네

그토록 오랜 세월
고운 꿈 가꾸며
이 밤도 잔잔한 강마을
창가에 쉬네.

RIVER VILLAGE

The village where my love lives
is the village where the sailboat arrives
and the warm heart resides
the river village of Willow Forest.

She lets the sun that rises from the hill
rest atop her head,
her delicate hands clasped together.
Endlessly, endlessly,
the heart waits.

The flocks of seagulls have left
after purging the suffering heart.
The sunset stains the blue river.

The longing heart desires
a field of white sand and reeds,
endlessly, endlessly.

When the lonely crescent moon
arrives at my window,
the little bird stops crying
and flies into the forest.

The quiet river village rests
at my window tonight,
as it safeguards my beautiful dream
for all eternity.

강의 노래

너와 나는
머언 후일
강(江)물로 만나자.

굽이 굽이
인생 굽이를
사랑처럼 맴돌다가

폭포를 만나면
함께 뛰어 내리고
여울을 지날 때엔
소리 높여 울어가자.

달빛이 쏟아지는
은모랫벌에서 피워내는
바람의 축제.

갈대들의
환호를 받으면서
기인
여정이 끝나는 포구에
해조음이
그리운 사람들의 발소리로
몰려 오며는

너와 나는
머언 후일
붉은
강(江)노을로 뜨자.

SONG OF THE RIVER

In the distant future,
let us meet at the river.
Twisting, turning life is turning like love.
When we meet at the waterfall,
we will leap together.

When we pass by the turbulence,
let us cry out loudly.

The song of the wind
is over the silvery sand dunes,
colored by the pouring moonlight.

The reeds give acclamation and cheers
as my long journey ends at the pier.
The music of the sea
arrives like people' s welcoming footsteps.

In the future, let us appear
like a colorful sunset on the river.

구름

누구의 마음입니까
해돋이 푸른 산자락에
붉게 물드는 구름은.

삶이 아무리 허망할지라도
그리운 얼굴
정든 사람들을 사랑하며 살기엔
가슴 벅찬
이 감격
이 만남.

버거운 하루가 다하고
또 하나의 내일이 약속되는
이 저녁

서산 마루에
소리 없이 젖어드는 장미빛 노을은
누구의 애타는 염원
간절한 기도입니까.

오늘도
님의 꿈으로 물드는
저문 하늘을 바라보며

착하고
아름답게 살기엔
자족한 하루입니다.

CLOUD

Whose heart is this?
The cloud dyed in red by the sunrise
on the lower edge of the mountain

Even though life is so meaningless,
to remember those yearning faces,
to love those who have been loved!

The heart overflows with deep emotion
from this meeting.

A hard day passes,
and another tomorrow is promised
this evening.

The rose-colored sunset
silently soaks into the mountain.

Whose sorrowful wish is this?
Whose sincere prayer?

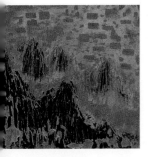

Today again,
I look at the sky dyed
by my lover's dream.

It is the day of self-sufficiency,
to love an honest and beautiful
life.

유채꽃

닫혔던 하늘이 문을 열면
그대의 손길처럼 부드러운
강언덕 위에
그리운 발길들이 몰려와
초록물감을 푼다.

여기 저기서
끝없이 흔들어대는 손길들

바람이 멎어도
가슴이 떨리고
굳었던 마음이 금시
황금물결로 출렁인다.

오월 언덕에는
그리운 사람은 그리움으로
애타는 사람은 심한 갈증으로
슬픈 사람은
꽃잎 같은 눈물로 섰을 일이다.

동구밖
유채밭에 나서면
사랑하는 사람들의
눈길들은
온통 금모래빛이다.

낮에는
땅에서 별빛으로
밤에는 하늘에서 꽃보라로
피어오르는 유채꽃.

끝없이 흔들어대던
그 손길 못잊어
바람이 멎어도
가슴이 떨리고
굳었던 마음이 금시
황금물결로 출렁인다.

RAPE FLOWER

As the sky opens its closed door,
yearning, we come and release our green dyes
onto your soft open hand like the river hill.

Waving outstretched hands endlessly,
everywhere

My heart shakes
though the wind stops,
and suddenly waves as a golden stream.

In the hills of May,
yearning, the sorrowful people
come with severe thirst,
with flowing tears like flower pellets.

Outside of the village,
people only look to the field of rape flowers
and golden sands.

During the day,
the light of stars blossom on the ground.
During the night,
a halo of flowers blossom in the sky.

Because I couldn' t forget,
waving outstretched hands endlessly,

everywhere
My heart shakes
though the wind stops,
and suddenly waves as a golden stream.

석류

타는 바람
흙먼지
한여름을
삭정이 울가에 서서
목마를 세월들

낙엽이 쌓이는
고궁 돌계단을
오르는 심정으로

가슴을 열어
임을 부르는
속마음은
루비빛 열정인데

기인 언덕
실개천에 늘어선
포플라 머리 위로
청량히 고이는
하늘은 자수정

이제
머언 길을 떠난
그대가
상념의 낙엽을 밟고
되돌아와

석류 같은
입술을 포개어
사랑을 입맞출 때

귓전에 흘러드는
그리움의 강물소리

지금은
우리 모두가
남기고 떠나온
고향 울가에 서서
타는 가슴을 열어
붉게 익을 석류여.

POMEGRANATE TREE

Burning wind
Dust from the dirt
Standing in the dry wooded wall
in mid-summer
Thirsting

As if I am climbing
the stone steps of the old palace
piled high with autumn leaves

My heart that is opened
to call out to my lover
is the color of ruby.

The amethyst sky is collecting
above the poplar lined against
the stream on the hill.

Now you are returning from the long trip,
stepping on leaves of ideals.

When I exchange a kiss of love
with your lips of pomegranate

the water sound of the river flows
into my ears.
It should still be standing

by the hometown brook that we left behind
and opening its burning heart
O, ripening red pomegranate tree!

가을 백사장

누가 걸어갔나
은빛 모래밭
외줄기
기인 발자국.

언제 떠나갔나
자국마다 고인
애수哀愁

가슴을 두드리는
저문 파도소리.

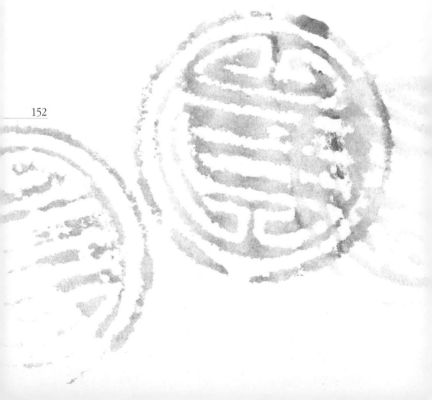

AUTUMN BEACH

Who walked by?
On the silvery sand
is a single line
of long footsteps.

When did he leave?
I see that each step
is stagnant with sorrow.

The sound of the crashing waves
pounds my heart.

낙화落花

늦은 봄날
울 밑에 잠든
삽살개 잔등 위로
솔솔이는 실바람.

나무 그늘을 지나는
여인의 옷깃에
꽃물결 무늬가
일고 있다.

지금은
어느 계집아이의
어머니가 되었을
세월인데

뒷집 아이가 날린
연鳶이
높이 떠올라
이별이 아픈
골목길.

시들은 꽃을 버리고

떠나가는
나비의 몸짓으로
낙화가 일고 있다.

머얼리서는
추억이 슬픈
강물소리.

그대와 함께 거닐던
거리에
꽃노을이 붉은
이 저녁

몸살을 앓아
수척해진
너의 모습이
무척 그립다.

FALLING FLOWERS

Late Spring.
The gently rising breeze
ruffled the fur of the dog
sleeping at the foot of the fence.

Waves of falling flowers
weaved into the clothes of the lovers
walking by under the shadow
of the tree.

By now,
the female lover must herself
be the mother of a girl.

The road is a memory
of a painful parting
marked by the child in the back house
flying a kite high.

Falling flowers wave
in the figure of a butterfly
that leaves a wilted
flower behind.

Far, far away,
is the sound of the river
with sorrowful memories.

The flower sunset
reddens this evening
in the street where I used to
walk with you.

I so miss the shape
of your thinning figure
heavy with fatigue.

카네이션

새하얀 유리컵에
긴 목을 들어내고
화사하게
웃는 얼굴.

창밖 흰눈이
엄동을 알리건만
북풍을 살라마셔
청초한 자태여

너도
내 마음을 알아
그토록 연연히
사모곡을 부르는가.

CARNATION

From a glass as clear as crystal
juts the smiling face
of a lovely carnation
atop its slender neck.

Even though the white snow
outside the window
reflects the winter,
when the north wind inhales
the flower, the image
is clean and blue.

You understand my heart
and sing a love song for me.

옥수수

어머님이
방문 가방에 넣어
전해주신
옥수수 씨앗
정이 그리워
울 가에 심었더니

한여름
낯선 하늘 우러르며 자라
간 밤

아기를 낳아
등에 업고
이른 아침
웃으며 서 있다

오. 오.
나를 등에 업고 계신
어머님.

CORN

My mother
brought the seed corn
in her travel bag
and gave it to me.
So, I planted it by the fence,
longing for her affection.

In mid-summer
it grew
looking up at the foreign sky,
and bore children
and carried them on its back,
standing and smiling
in the early morning.

Oh, oh
my mother
who carries me on her back.

발렌타인스 데이

박꽃같이 소박한
눈송이들이
언 가지 위에
꽃으로 피어나는

이월 열나흘
발렌타인스의 날이 오면

상수리나무에
햇잎 돋듯
그리운 생각들이
가득히 번져

사랑하고픈 그를 위하여
사랑하는 임을 위하여
사랑하였던 옛날을 회상하며

목 가눠
가슴 터지는 석류같이
붉은 장미 꽃다발을
건네주면서
내일을 약속하는
그리움의 손길들……

사랑은
낭랑한 물결이라
눈을 감아도 흘러들고

사랑은
은빛 햇살이라
창을 닫아도 새어드네

사랑은
귀를 막아도
낯익은 음성으로
살아 되돌아와

문을 두드리는
영원의 메아리.

이제 나는
너를 향한
한 그루의 따가운 장미이려니

너는
내게로 와서
한 떨기 꽃이 되렴
그윽한 향이 되렴

거리엔
차가운 가슴 가슴을 찾아가
사랑의 불을 지피는
발렌타인스 후예들의
그리운 발소리.

VALENTINE' S DAY

Snowflakes
as naive as a gourd flower
blossom on the frozen branch.

It is the 14th of February,
when Valentine' s Day arrives.

The yearning heart spreads
over the acorn tree
like a fresh bud.

For whom I want to love
For whom I love
Remembering the times when I used to love

Hands of yearning
carry over a bunch of red roses
like a pomegranate about to burst.

Because love is a lively stream
it comes in even though eyes are closed.

Because love is a silver sunshine
it comes in even though the window is closed.

Love
comes back as a low tone

even though the ear is closed.

The eternal echo
knocks on the door.

I am now the stem of a thorny rose,
bent towards you.

You come to me and
become a stem of a flower,
become a secluded fragrance.

On the street are the yearning sounds
of people' s footsteps on Valentine' s Day,
burning a fire of love,
searching for a cold mind.

장미밭에서

잠든 영혼이 눈을 뜨는
이른 아침
장미의 뜨락을 거닐면
소록소록 마음을 열며
피어오르는 사랑의 숨결.

더러는
눈길로 말하고
더러는
향기로 부르며

삶의 진실과 번뇌를 고백하는
여신의 숲엔
생명의 늪으로 빨려드는
무수한 영혼의
빛과 소리들……

인간이 저만큼
아름다울 수 있다면
초연할 수 있다면
여유로 설 수 있다면

짝을 맞아
가슴 떨리는 연인을 위하여
라반다의 진한 향기를

병상에서 새로운 삶을 다짐하는
아픈 마음을 위하여
브라이델 와이트의
청초함을……

사랑하는 모두를

남기고 떠나는

임의 관 위엔
불같이 타오르는
로얄티 붉은 장미를
승리의 축가처럼 덮어드리거라.

생일의 기쁨을 맞이하는 그대에겐
황금빛 엠브름을

영광의 졸업을 맞는 자녀들에게는
핑크의 여왕
바비의 꽃다발을

한 해의 삶을 감사드리는
추수의 계절엔
앤젤리퀘 오렌지빛
장미의 향기를

마음과
정성과
가슴에 담아
드리오리라.

인간이 저만큼
아름다울 수 있다면
초연할 수 있다면
여유로 설 수 있다면

잠든 영혼이 눈을 뜨는 아침
장미의 뜨락엔
소록소록 가슴을 열며
흘러드는 영원의 숨결.

FIELD OF ROSES

The sleeping soul opens its eyes
in the early morning.
Walking around the rose garden,
I calmly open up my mind.
The breath of love is blossoming.

Sometimes I speak to you through my eyes.
Sometimes I call you through my scent.

The Goddess in the forest confesses the truth and
agony of life,
the countless lights and sounds of the soul
which are absorbed into life.

What if humans could be as beautiful and calm and
holy
as the Goddess in the forest
and live as she does?

Finding a mate -
a sweetheart who makes the heart tremble -
the promise of the deep scent of lavender

To a painful heart at the sickbed
longing for a new life -
the promise of the tidiness of bridal white

On top of the coffin of the one
who is leaving all loved ones behind,
the promise of royal red roses that burn like fire

Let it be covered
like a celebration of a victory.
The golden emblem is for you
whose birthday is greeted by happiness.

To the children who are greeted
by the glory of graduation-
queen of pink,
bouquet of Barbie

For the harvest season,
when we give thanks
for the life of the year-
the fragrance of the angelic
orange roses

빨래

아내가
맑은 물에 헹궈
깨끗이 다려준
옷을 입고
세상 속으로 나간다.

바람이 불고
먼지가 일고
눈비가 오고
요설饒舌이 난무하는
스산한 음지陰地

세심정혼洗心淨魂의 마음으로
정결淨潔해야 할 옷깃에
온갖 때가 달라붙는다.

박꽃 같은 마음으로
문을 나서
구겨진 빨래감으로
되돌아 오는 일상日常

오늘도
하늘에는
아침 이슬로 씻긴
한 줄기 구름이
어머님의 손길로 바래진
옥양목같이
희게 걸려 있다.

LAUNDRY

I wear
the clothes that my wife
cleaned in the clear water
and ironed,
and go out into the world.

The wind blows,
the dust rises,
the snow and rains come-
the chatter of the masses
in the dark world.

With a clear heart,
the collar that should be clean
becomes stained with dirt.

With a heart like a gold flower,
I go out
and I return with wrinkled laundry.
O my every day!

Once again today
in the sky,
a line of clouds
washed by the morning dew
hangs whitely,
like the calico that has been faded
by my mother's touch.

가을 달

바람이
알몸으로 거리에 나서는
늦가을.

산은
수줍어
얼굴 붉히고

철없이
속살 들어내는
가을 강
그윽한 물결.

고향의 전설처럼
평과주가 익어 가는
외진 산마을.

울 가
대 소리도
사각사각
서릿발을 빚는데

창가 고목에 걸린
차가운 달을 품으니

그대 그리워
눈물 어리네.

* 평과주 : 사과주

AUTUMN MOON

The wind reveals
its naked body in the street
in the late Autumn.

The mountain
turns red
from embarrassment.

The innocent Autumn river
reveals its body.
Tranquil river.

Like a legend in my hometown,
the wine ripens
in the lonely mountain village.

The ringing of the bamboo
at the fence
combs the crispy frost.

I embrace the cold moon
that is hanging
off the old tree by the window.
Longing for you,
the tears well up.

가을 풍경

간 밤
별빛이
유난히 차게 밝더니
계곡에는
무서리가 내리고

돌배나무 잎이
자지러지게 무르익어
지나던 길손도
취하여 조는데

들길을 지나는 바람이
피리소리가 되어
저무는 이 저녁

기인 산 그늘이
주막에 붐비네.

행낭을 밀고 가는
배달부 발길에도
정든 사람들의
숨결이 가득한데

고령산 보광사
타는 단풍이
옷깃에 배어

얼굴과
가슴이 붉던
내 소녀는

지금
어느 길목에서
그리움에 취하여
잠을 청하는가.

AUTUMN SCENERY

In the midst of the night
the stars are extremely bright.
The first frost of the year
has fallen in the valley.

The wild pear leaves are so
heavy with ripe fruit,
that those passing by
are intoxicated by the sight.

The passing wind turns into
the sound of a flute,
and the night is getting
deeper.

The lengthening shadows
cast by the mountain
crowd together at the
inn below.

The footsteps of the mail carrier
who is pushing his cart
contains the breath of
peoples' affection.

At the Bo Kwang temple
of the Ko Ryung mountains,

the burning Autumn leaves
soak the hem of my clothing.

With rosy cheeks and warm heart,
My girl-

Right now,
at which road are you asking
for a moment to rest, drunk
from longing?

치악산雉岳山

산이 좋아
산을 오르네.

그리움에 취하여 오르는 산길
그 마음 못 잊어
달도 따라 나서고

산심山心을 싣고
세렴폭포 뛰어내려
달려오는 시냇물도
나를 반겨 맞는데

흐르다 쉬어가는 맑은 소沼에는
구룡사龜龍寺 선경禪景이
병풍을 두르고
그대 마음이 애틋이 고여 있네.

세속의 번뇌를
아득히 잊고
치악산 비로봉을
오르는 산행

간밤 찬서리에
타는 연정戀情으로
잎마다 저리 붉어
옷깃에 젖어드네.

CHI-AHK MOUNTAIN

Since I enjoy the mountain,
I climb it.

Drunken with yearning,
I climb the mountain road.
Because it can' t forget
its heart, the moon is
following me too.

The water from the stream,
filled with the love of the mountain,
travels down the stream
to greet me.

At the clear swamp,
where the running stream is resting,
beautiful scenes of the Goo-Ryong
Temple surround it,
and your heart is dwelling in it.

Forgetting all the worldly agony,
climbing to the Bee-Ryoh mountaintop,
leaves like color of passion
are wetting my sleeve
like the frost at night.

구곡폭포*

일곡에 서린 하늘빛
이곡에 피는 꽃구름
삼곡에 내리는 안개비
사곡에 번지는 청솔향
오곡에 흐르는 산바람
육곡에 피어오르는 물보라
칠곡에 솟아나는 무지개
팔곡에 낭랑한 님의 음성
구곡에 떠 있는 님 그림자.

아득히 깊은 계곡에는 그리움이 넘치는데
님을 부르면 나는 그대를 사랑해요
아홉 마디로 아롱져 가슴을 두드리는
구곡폭포.

얼마나 그리우면
저리 급히 달려오나
밤에도 낮에도 님 그리워

애타게 내려 쏟는
구곡폭포.

연인을 부르는
사랑의 메아리로 타오르는
붉은 산 노을.

* 경기 가평 북한강변의 폭포

GU GOK WATERFALL

Hanging beams of sky at the first curve
Blossoming flower cloud at the second curve
Falling foggy rain at the third curve
Spreading pine tree fragrance at the fourth curve
Flying mountain wind at the fifth curve
Sprouting water spray at the sixth curve
Rising rainbow at the seventh curve
Echoing lover' s voice at the eighth curve
Floating lover' s shadow at the ninth curve

There is yearning, flooding
at the deep valley.
I call out to you, my dear,
"I love you."
It is mottled in nine curves
and pounds my heart at Gu Gok waterfall.

How full of yearning you are.
You run into me so quickly
all night and during the day,
yearning for your lover,
showering sadly at Gu Gok waterfall.

Calling out for your lover
Burning a tune of love
Red mountain sunset

용문사龍門寺

기氣가 솟아
산이 되고
한恨이 서려
바위가 되는가

섬섬옥수纖纖玉手
낙랑공주의 손길을
뿌리치고
마의麻衣를 두른 채
금강산 가는 길에 꽂았다는
태자의 지팡이가
저리도 정정히 버텨
천년세월 황금빛인데

옛 님이 그리워
백발노안白髮老顔
정인情人의 손을 잡고
산길을 오르는
그대의 마음은

바람인가
구름인가
달빛인가

연지볼 타는 단풍으로
물든 산 노을.

그리워라
앳된 얼굴

꿈에라도
자로자로 드소서

이 밤도
가슴을 파고드는
그리운 물결소리.

YONG—MUN TEMPLE

The Chi rises
into a mountain,
and the Han forms
into a rock.

On the way to Kum-Kang Mountain,
shaking off Princess Naklang's
beautiful and sad hands,
the Prince, MaouiTaeja, planted
a tree that has endured vigorously
to bear golden leaves.

Missing the old lover and
holding the beloved's hand and
climbing to a mountain path,
you, with the old face
and white hair,

are the wind
or the cloud
or the moon's ray.

The sunset glows like a maple,
burning like the cheek's rouge.

Missing you,
a face like a child's

often comes to me
even in my dream.

Tonight
the sound of yearning waves
is engraved in my heart.

겨울 달

빈 산 가득
은빛 물결에 씻긴 옷소매가
옥이요 학이로구나.

알몸인 저 달
홀로 달아오르는데
찻잔에 서려오는
정인情人의 애틋한 마음

설원雪源을 달려
영嶺을 넘는 솔바람
피리를 불고

처마 끝 풍경소리
님의 발소린 양
문을 두드리네.

날 저물어
길 험한 이 밤
그대 지금
어느 길녘에서
찬 눈을 맞는가

이제
밤은 깊은 삼경
타는 꿈길 엮으러
달님처럼 오소서.

WINTER MOON

The sleeves that have been
washed by the silvery water,
filled in the empty mountains-
it is the jade,
it is the crane

The moon is a naked body
rising up all alone
The sweetheart's affection
is gathering in a cup

The wind that runs through
the snowfield, climbing over
the mountaintop, is playing
the flute

The sound of the wind chime
at the edge of the roof
is like your footsteps knocking
on the doors

As the day is over
and the road is rough tonight,
from which road are you
greeting the cold snow?

Now,
the dream that fell
deep into midnight
arrives like a moon

가로등街路燈

어두움이
싸락눈처럼
거리에 덮여 오면
연인의 눈빛 같은
가로등들이
하나 둘
눈을 뜨기 시작한다.

팔짱을 끼고 걷는
조용한 발소리
그 속삭임이
달빛 같이 고요하다.

만나면 만날수록
샘솟는 그리움

늘어선 가로등을 따라
연인들이
정겹게 걸어 가고 있다

그들의
가슴이 따스한
이 저녁.

STREET LIGHT

When the darkness covers the streets like a pile of
snow,
the street lights open their eyes one by one.

The sound of quiet footsteps with arms linked
that whisper is the silence of the moon.

The more I see you,
the feeling of missing you slowly rises.

Following the street lights that are stretched out,
lovers are friendlily walking.

Their hearts are warm
this evening.

김난옥金蘭玉

아호 시연詩然 / 경희교육대학원 / 개인전 4회 / 대한민국 미술대전 입선 및 특선 / 무등미술대전 대상 / 인천시전 대상 / 목우회 입선 및 특선 / 국제 교류전 및 초대전 다수 / 국내 단체전 60여 회 참가 / 종로미술협회 이사, 서예진흥협회 이사 / 산채수묵회 회원, 구상회 회원 / 여성작가회 운영위원 / 도솔미술대전 심사위원장 역임 / 전남도전심사 / 각 미술단체 공모전 심사 / 수필집《마스카라 머리에 칠하고》출간

너를 향해 사랑의 연鳶을 띄운다
Flying A Love Kite For You

시 | 정용진
그림 | 김난옥

펴낸 이 | 임종대
펴낸 곳 | 미래문화사

찍은 날 | 2007년 3월 15일
펴낸 날 | 2007년 3월 20일

등록 번호 | 제3-44호
등록 일자 | 1976년 10월 19일
주소 | 서울시 용산구 효창동 5-421
전화 | 715-4507 / 713-6647
팩시밀리 | 713-4805
E-mail | miraebooks@korea.com
mirae715@hanmail.net
ⓒ 2007, 미래문화사
ISBN | 89-7299-330-1 03810

* 책 가격은 표지 뒷면에 있습니다.